Jodie's First Dig

By Anna Levine
Illustrated by Ksenia Topaz

KAR-BEN
PUBLISHING

For Judye Groner, editor and good friend, Beth Wagner Brust,
my wonderful writer-buddy, and for my family, who all share the love
of traveling "to far-off places." You are my source of inspiration. — A.L.

To my amazing daughters, who always stand by me, both as family and as
the most truthful reviewers of my work. — K.T.

Kar-Ben Publishing
A division of Lerner Publishing Group, Inc.
241 First Avenue North
Minneapolis, MN 55401 U.S.A.
Website address: www.karben.com

Library of Congress Cataloging-in-Publication Data

Levine, Anna.
    Jodie's Hanukkah Dig / by Anna Levine ; illustrated by Ksenia Topaz.
        p. cm.
    Summary: Jodie dreams of one day becoming a famous archaeologist and when her father takes her to visit a dig in Modi'in,
Israel, home of the Maccabees, she is uniquely able to help.
    ISBN 978-0-8225-7391-3 (lib. bdg. : alk. paper)
    [1. Archaeology–Fiction. 2. Hanukkah–Fiction. 3. Jews–Israel–Fiction. 4. Israel–Fiction.] I. Topaz, Ksenia, ill.
    II. Title.
    PZ7.L57823Jo 2008
    [E]–dc22 2007043134

Manufactured in the United States of America
1 2 3 4 5 6 – DP – 14 13 12 11 10 09

Jodie dreamed of being a famous archaeologist. She wanted to travel to far-off places, discover ancient lands, and uncover treasures hidden deep inside the earth. Just like her dad.

"You're too little," said her older brother Shimi. "Archaeologists use big tools."

"You're not strong enough," said her other brother Eli. "Archaeologists carry heavy loads of dirt."

"Maybe when you're older," said her mother, who was busy packing the boys' bags. It was vacation and they were going on a camping trip. "Shimi, where is your other shoe?"

"Buried inside the closet, maybe?" he answered.

Jodie crawled into the dark,
dusty depths of Shimi's closet.
"Found it!" she said.

"You do have keen eyesight,"
said Mother. "Stay here and
keep an eye on your dad while
I drive the boys to camp."

Jodie found her father in his study, with a pile of papers. "Daddy, can you take me to see the ruins at Pompeii?"

"Those are in Italy. That's far away. Why don't you read a book about them instead."

Jodie sighed. "How will I ever be a famous archaeologist if I never go on a dig? It's not enough to read about it. I want to feel the shovel in my hand, the sun on my head, and the–"

"Spiders?" asked Dad.

"Archaeologists aren't afraid of spiders," said Jodie.

"Tell you what," said Dad. "I can't take you to Pompeii, but Professor Hoffer is digging at the site where Judah Maccabee fought against the Syrians. He wants to show me what they've found. Let's go today!"

Jodie ran to pack up the car with shovels, pails, water bottles, and a snack.

Dad drove out of their neighborhood in Jerusalem,
down the hill, under the overpass and all the way to Modi'in.
He parked the car beside the sign that said:

Diggers this way. Watch your step.
Slip and you may fall back in time.

"Maybe I'll find Judah's sword or uncover a secret passage," Jodie said. She pointed to a group of people standing on a hill. "Look, Dad, they must be the diggers."

Jodie and her dad climbed up the hill until they found
Professor Hoffer, a tall man with big, broad shoulders and
a green, floppy hat. He waved them over.

"This is my daughter Jodie," said Dad. "She wants to be an archaeologist. We're here to see what you've found."

"A very unusual hole," said the professor. Tossing off his hat, he stuck his head inside the hole. He wiggled in one shoulder and then tried to wiggle in the other.

"*Gharekghitwehkretitnh!*" he shouted.

"What did he say?" asked Jodie.

"I think he means that we should pull him out," said Dad.

Once Professor Hoffer was right side up, he said, "It looks as if this might be very interesting. But I can't get in far enough to know for sure. The hole is very narrow, and the light doesn't reach. But if we dig a bigger hole, it might cave in."

While the professor and Jodie's dad thought about what to do next, Jodie wandered over to the volunteers.

The line of diggers passing pails of dirt snaked all the way around the hill.

"Would you like to join the bucket brigade?" one of them asked.

Jodie picked up a shovel and started to dig. The sun burned fiercely.

The dirt kept piling up. Each shovelful felt heavier than the one before.

"Archaeology is very hard work," she said to herself.

She stopped to take a break, and walked back to her dad and Professor Hoffer.

"If only I were younger, a bit smaller, and my eyes were sharper," said the professor, "then I could see inside the hole."

That gave Jodie an idea. She tapped him on the shoulder. "Excuse me, Professor. I know of an archaeologist who is younger, smaller, and has very sharp eyes."

"And who might that be?" he asked.

"Me!" said Jodie.

"You're too small to be on a dig," he answered.

"I'm small enough to fit in a bucket so you can lower me into the hole. I can be your eyes. My dad has taught me all about archaeology," she persisted. "I'll know if I see something important."

"I don't know," said the professor.

"Let's give her a chance," said Dad.

Jodie climbed inside the bucket before they could change their minds. The professor strapped a rope around her waist to keep her safe. He gave her a flashlight and said, "I hope you're not afraid of spiders."

"Spiders?" She gulped. "Archaeologists aren't afraid of spiders."

Slowly, they lowered her into the hole. As the bucket bumped and swayed, the air got damper and everything turned darker. Jodie's flashlight did little to light up the cave. "I'm not afraid of the dark," Jodie reminded herself.

The musty air made her sneeze. The sound echoed off the walls. "And I'm not afraid of bad smells and loud noises."

Something brushed against her arm. She swept it away and swallowed her shriek. "And I'm not afraid of spiders!"

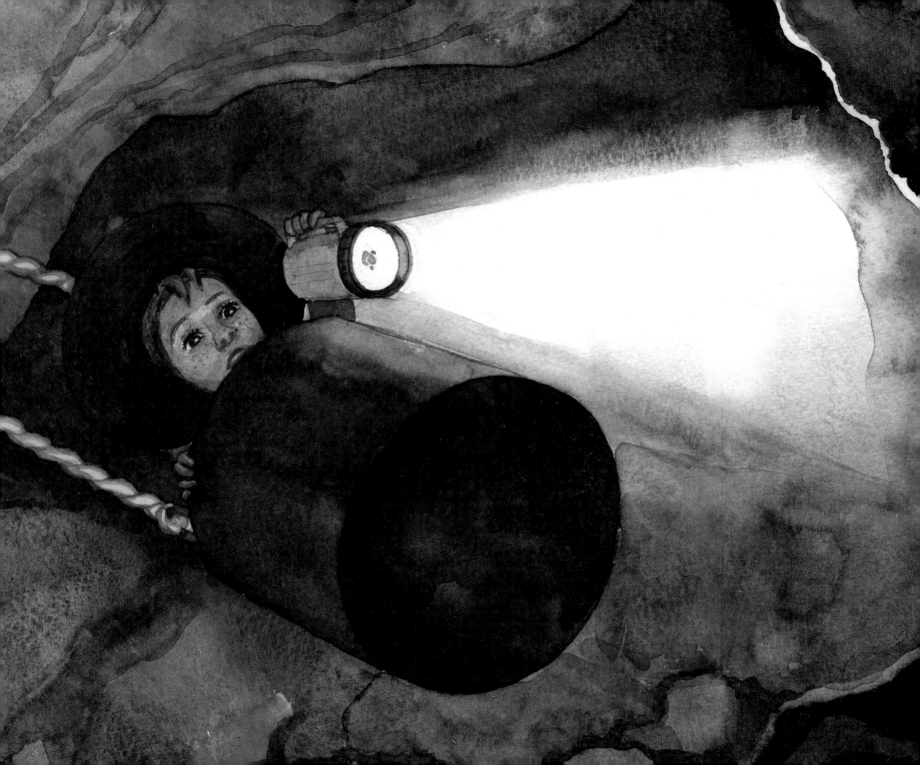

Jodie's bucket landed with a bump.
The cave was cool and quiet. Flashing her light
first left and then right, she decided it was safe enough
to step out.

"What do you see?" the professor called down to her.

Jodie brushed her fingers against the walls. "The sides are
soft and the color of vanilla ice cream."

"Limestone or chalk. Just as I thought," the professor said.

"It looks like someone has dug out an alleyway," Jodie continued.
"I think I can crawl through here."

"Not this time," said Dad. "We're going to bring you back up."

"Back in the bucket, please!"
said the professor.
    They tugged on the bucket
and Jodie leaped inside.

"Tell us all you saw," said the professor, as they helped her out.

"It looked like a maze of underground passageways," she reported.

"So there must be another entrance farther on," said the professor.

"Anything else?"

Jodie opened her tighly clenched fist.

"And this," she said, holding out her hand.

"We can't see what she has," said the students, gathering around.

Professor Hoffer hoisted Jodie up on his tall broad shoulders.

"An arrowhead!" shouted one.

"From the time of Judah Maccabee?" asked another.

"Could be," said the professor. "How do you think the Maccabees got all the way down there?"

Jodie smiled. "They must have been nimble enough to crawl through the tiny passageways, brave enough not to be afraid of the dark, and strong enough to fight off all the people who thought they were too little to win."

"Just like my Jodie," said Dad.

They said good-bye to Professor Hoffer, walked back down the hill, drove over the underpass and all the way back to Jerusalem, where Mother was waiting for them.